AF584430

Famous Australians

# Australian Children's Authors

Rachel Dixon

First published 2017 by
Redback Publishing
PO Box 357 Frenchs Forest NSW 2086
Australia



ISBN 978-1-9256301-6-9



Author: Rachel Dixon
Editor: Jane Tara
Original illustrations © Redback Publishing 2017
Originated by Redback Publishing
Printed and bound in China by Leo Paper

MIX
Paper from responsible sources
FSC
www.fsc.org
FSC® C020056

Acknowledgements
Abbreviations: l—left, r—right, b—bottom, t—top, c—centre, m—middle
We would like to thank the following for permission to reproduce photographs:
Ubud Writers Festival and Stefan Tell via Wikimedia Commons, p4b Norman Lindsay 1921 by Harold Cazneaux gelatin silver photograph Collection: National Portrait Gallery, Canberra Gift of Richard King 2008 Donated through the Australian Government's Cultural Gifts Program. p5 Ethel Turner 1928 By Harold Cazneaux gelatin silver photograph Collection: National Portrait Gallery, Canberra Gift of Richard King 2008 Donated through the Australian Government's Cultural Gifts Program, p9 © Pamela Allen, p18 By Ubud Writers Festival [CC BY 2.0 (http://creativecommons.org/licenses/by/2.0)], via Wikimedia Commons, p27 - By Stefan Tell (mynewsdesk) [CC BY 3.0 (http://creativecommons.org/licenses/by/3.0)], via Wikimedia Commons

Every effort has been made to contact copyright holders of any material reproduced in this book. Any omissions will be rectified in subsequent printings if notice is given to the publisher.



National Library of Australia Cataloguing-in-Publication entry

Creator: Dixon, Rachel, author.
Title: Australian children's authors / Rachel Dixon.
ISBN: 9781925630169 (hardback)
Series: Famous Australians.
Target Audience: For primary school age.
Subjects: Authors, Australian--Biography.
Children's literature, Australian.

# Contents

# Australian Children's Authors

## 1800s to early 1900s

### May Gibbs (1877 - 1969)

May Gibbs was born in England and moved to Perth when she was four years old. Her stories about the Gumnut Babies and the Banksia Men were some of the first to use the Australian bush as a source of inspiration for characters in children's books. She began her career as a journalist and illustrator and published her first book in 1916. As well as writing stories, May Gibbs also drew cartoons for newspapers, featuring her characters Bib and Bub, and Tiggy Touchwood. These were published weekly over many years. May Gibb's house, Nutcote, in Sydney, is now a museum where visitors can see the bush surroundings that feature in many of her stories. When talking about the garden she said, "...that's where I got my best ideas." In 1955, she was awarded an MBE for services to literature.

**Books by May Gibbs include:**

Gum Blossom Babies
Gumnut Babies
Boronia Babies
Flannel Flowers and Other Bush Babies
Wattle Babies
Snugglepot and Cuddlepie
Bib and Bub
The Further Adventures of Bib and Bub

### Norman Lindsay (1879 – 1969)

Norman Lindsay, one of Australia's most famous artists, also wrote the classic children's story The Magic Pudding about an angry Christmas pudding that can talk and never disappears, no matter how much of it is eaten. Renowned for the exotic subjects of his paintings, Norman Lindsay's story characters are laughable caricatures that poke fun at human nature.

**Books by Norman Lindsay include:**

The Magic Pudding
The Flyaway Highway

### Ethel Turner (1872 - 1958)

Ethel Turner's children's stories about the Woolcot family, their tragedies, adventures and lives, were amongst the first novels set in Australia with children who were recognisably Australian in their manners, language and ideas. Seven Little Australians has become an Australian classic.

**Books by Ethel Turner include:**

Seven Little Australians
The Family at Misrule
Judy and Punch
The Little Larrikin

### Ethel Pedley (1859 - 1898)

Ethel Pedley was a musician who set up the first system of formal music examinations in Australia. She also wrote Dot and the Kangaroo about a little girl who gets lost in the bush and learns about the animals and their lives from a kangaroo. This work was unusual for the time as it had a talking Australian animal as a character.

**Book by Ethel Pedley:**

Dot and the Kangaroo

Above: Norman Lindsay
Right: Ethel Turner

# Australian Children's Authors

## mid 1900s

### Nan Chauncy (1900 - 1970)

Nan Chauncy began writing books for children at a time when Australian settings and characters were not common in children's literature. In Tangara and Mathinna's People she wrote about Aboriginal issues, which was groundbreaking for the time.

**Books by Nan Chauncy include:**

Tiger in the Bush
Devil's Hill
Tangara
They Found a Cave
Mathinna's People

### Ruth Park (1917 - 2010)

Ruth Park was born in New Zealand and later lived in Australia. As the editor of a children's section in a newspaper, she learned what sorts of books children really enjoy, and used this knowledge to write stories about life in Australia.

**Books by Ruth Park include:**

Playing Beatie Bow
The Muddle-Headed Wombat series

### Colin Thiele (1920 - 2006)

Colin Thiele's books for children are mostly set in the rural areas of his childhood. His most well-known story is Storm Boy, about a friendship between a boy and an injured pelican. The novel was made into a movie in 1976. Colin Thiele was also a teacher and school Principal.

**Books by Colin Thiele include:**

Storm Boy
Blue Fin
The Fire in the Stone
The Valley Between
Fiery Salamander

### Dorothy Wall (1894 - 1942)

Famous in Australia as the creator of the Blinky Bill character, Dorothy Wall was also an illustrator of many other books for children by different authors. She loved the Australian bush and wrote the Blinky Bill stories to amuse her own son.

**Books by Dorothy Wall include:**

Tommy Bear and the Zookies
Blinky Bill
Blinky Bill Grows Up
Blinky Bill and Nutsy

### Patricia Wrightson (1921 - 2010)

Patricia Wrightson set her children's stories in Australia, with indigenous influences and local themes. She was one of the first children's novelists in Australia to take this course and was therefore a trailblazer in her choice of subjects and settings. She was a CBCA winner and was also awarded the international Hans Christian Andersen Award.

**Books by Patricia Wrightson include:**

The Nargun and the Stars
The Crooked Snake
The Ice is Coming
I Own the Racecourse

#### HANS CHRISTIAN ANDERSEN AWARD

An international award for children's literature. The only Australian author to win this award was Patricia Wrightson in 1986.

Right: Patricia Wrightson

# TIMELINE

## Children's Literature in Australia

### Before 1788

Dreaming stories are important spiritual and community tales that Aboriginal children learn.

### Early 1800s

Children's books from Britain set out rules for how children should behave.

### Late 1800s

Stories written for Australian children begin to have rebellious characters who don't always do the right thing. Aboriginal stories are retold by colonial writers.

### Early 1900s

Local writers use the Australian bush and its animals as a source of inspiration for the creation of new characters.

### 1945

The Children's Book Council of Australia is formed and begins to influence the style of local children's literature.

### 1960s

Free public libraries start making children's books more accessible for everyone.

### Late 1900s

Picture books and novels for teenagers become very popular.

# Australian Children's Authors

## late 1900s to the present

### Emma Allen

Emma Allen's very first picture book, The Terrible Suitcase, won a CBCA Award. Her stories are about the things that can upset children when they first start school, and how they can find ways to overcome them.

**Books by Emma Allen include:**

The Terrible Suitcase
My Friend Ernest

### Pamela Allen

Born in New Zealand, Pamela Allen has most of her books published in Australia, where she is the winner of numerous awards. Her stories have a musical and theatrical quality that makes them perfect for storytime reading.

**Books by Pamela Allen include:**

Mr McGee series
Mr Archimedes' Bath
Who Sank the Boat?
Bertie and the Bear

### Allan Baillie

Allan Baillie was born in Scotland and moved to Australia when he was seven years old. His writing ranges from being light-hearted and humorous, to serious and political. In The China Coin and Rebel, he places his young characters at the centre of violent and tumultuous world events.

**Books by Allan Baillie include:**

The China Coin
Treasure Hunters
Little Brother
Saving Abbey
Krakatoa Lighthouse
Drac and the Gremlin
Rebel

Left: © Pamela Allen

## Jeannie Baker

Jeannie Baker set a new standard in picture books with her beautifully detailed collage art. Her topics are about nature, spaces for living and the importance of ecology, even in cities.

**Books by Jeannie Baker include:**
Where the Forest Meets the Sea
Mirror
Belonging
The Hidden Forest
Window

## Aaron Blabey

Aaron Blabey writes picture books and stories for children. The characters are humorous, sometimes eccentric and scary, and always seem to be in a state of surprise at finding themselves in unusual situations.

**Books by Aaron Blabey include:**
Bad Guys series
Pig the Pug series
Piranhas Don't Eat Bananas
The Brothers Quibble
The Ghost of Miss Annabel Spoon

## Nick Bland

Nick Bland writes picture books with outrageous and hilarious characters. In The Wrong Book characters jostle and try to take over, while in his Bear series a big brown bear is constantly trying to work out how to do things that bears don't normally do.

**Books by Nick Bland include:**
The Wrong Book
The Very Cranky Bear
The Very Brave Bear
The Runaway Hug
A Monster Wrote Me a Letter

Right: Aaron Blabey
Below: Nick Bland

# PARTS OF A BOOK

*Did you know that every section of a book has a special name?*

## Title Page

The page with the title and author printed on it.

## Spine

The part down the side where the pages are glued or sewn together.

## Verso

Left hand pages.

## Recto

Right hand pages.

## End Paper

The pages at both ends of a book that are not part of the text.

## Leaf

Each single piece of paper in a book.

## Gutter

The space in the middle between two pages.

## Spread

Two pages laid out flat together.

## Anna Branford

Anna Branford's novels for children have gentle stories featuring children and elves working out what to do when faced by life's small dilemmas.

**Books by Anna Branford include:**

Lily the Elf series
Violet Mackerel series

## Isobelle Carmody

Best known for her fantasy stories for children and teenagers, Isobelle Carmody started writing her first novel in the Obernewtyn series when she was still at school, and has taken forty-three years to produce the final instalment.

**Books by Isobelle Carmody include:**

The Obernewtyn Chronicles series
The Gathering
Greylands
The Legend of Little Fur series
The Kingdom of the Lost series

## Judith Clarke

A writer of coming-of-age stories for tweens and teens, Judith Clarke's novels are a sensitive and intense portrayal of the emotional turmoils of the teenage years. Her work has received many awards both in Australia and overseas.

**Books by Judith Clarke include:**

The Winds of Heaven
One Whole and Perfect Day
Three Summers
Wolf on the Fold
Al Capsella series
Night Train

## Gary Crew

Gary Crew writes stories for teenagers and picture books for young children. He has won the CBCA Awards for both of these categories.

**Books by Gary Crew include:**

Strange Objects
Angel's Gate
Quentaris series
Sam Silverthorne series

## Anh Do

Anh Do draws on his experiences as a Vietnamese refugee to craft stories that are both funny and poignant. His chapter books for young children are about the funny outcomes when a Vietnamese boy tries to understand and fit in with his Aussie classmates. Anh Do is also a comedian and a television personality.

**Books by Anh Do include:**

The Little Refugee
Hotdog series
WeirDo series

## Ursula Dubosarsky

Ursula Dubosarsky writes both fiction and non-fiction for children. Her novels and picture books do not fall into any one category and their variety of themes makes them fascinating for her fans.

**Books by Ursula Dubosarsky include:**

The Terrible Plop
Too Many Elephants in This House
The Cryptic Casebook of Coco Carlomagno series
The Word Spy

Above: Ursula Dubosarsky. Right: Isobelle Carmody, Inset: Anna Branford

# TYPES OF BOOKS

Children's books can be published in many different formats...

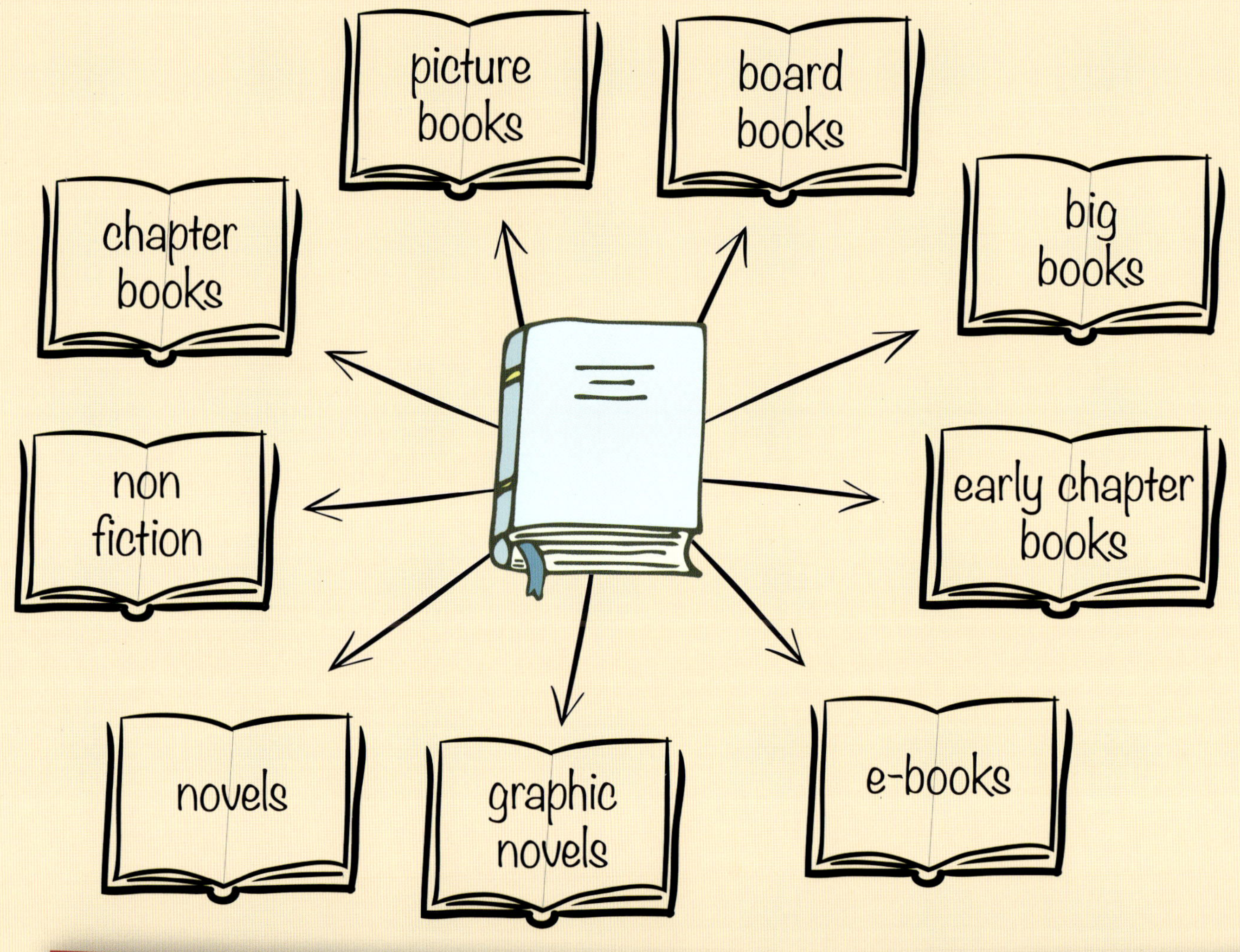


- Look in your school or public library to find examples of these types of books.
- Try choosing a book from two of these types and working out what makes their formats different. For example, a Big Book is produced in a very large size for reading to a room full of children. These books have big typefaces and pictures so that everyone can see them. In contrast, a graphic novel has small comic-style drawings that only one reader would be able to see clearly.
- Now think about the formats you would use to write a book of your own.
- What are the features and benefits of the format that you would choose?

## Lesley Gibbes

Lesley Gibbes is a teacher who also writes picture books and novels for young children. She encourages other writers to never give up and to keep practising every day. Her own Jack Russell Terriers were the inspiration for the Fizz series of chapter books about a fluffy little dog who wants to be a police dog.

**Books by Lesley Gibbes include:**

Scary Night
Fizz Series
Little Bear's First Sleep
Quick as a Wink, Fairy Pink
Bring a Duck!

## Mem Fox

Mem Fox's picture book, Possum Magic, has been popular ever since it was published in 1983. This title also won the first KOALA award in 1987. Ten Little Fingers and Ten Little Toes was given to Prince George, Queen Elizabeth's great-grandson, as Australia's official gift when he was born. Mem Fox is dedicated to children's literacy and is a retired Associate Professor of Literacy Studies.

**Books by Mem Fox include:**

Time for Bed
Where Is The Green Sheep?
Ten Little Fingers and Ten Little Toes
Possum Magic
Baby Bedtime
Goodnight Sleep Tight

Right: Jackie French
Above: Lesley Gibbes

## Jackie French

Jackie French writes picture books, non-fiction and novels for children. She was appointed the Australian Children's Laureate for 2014 and 2015 and also the Senior Australian of the Year in 2015. In 2016, she became a Member of the Order of Australia for her services to children's literature. She is the winner of a number of CBCA Awards, as well as many other awards from around the world. Jackie is dyslexic and passionate about the importance of reading for all children. Her best-selling Diary of a Wombat picture book draws on her own experiences looking after wombats. Jackie's novels reveal an interest in telling the ordinary person's story in Australian history, along with a concern for wildlife and nature. Her retellings of Shakespearean stories show how the characters are still relevant to young people today.

**Books by Jackie French include:**

Diary of a Wombat
Hitler's Daughter
The Girl from Snowy River
Ophelia
I Am Juliet

## Libby Gleeson

Libby Gleeson's books for children have received many accolades, including CBCA Book of the Year Awards. She has also written for the children's TV series, Bananas in Pyjamas. Beginning her career as a teacher, Libby Gleeson helps to train new teachers through her role as an Adjunct Associate Professor at the University of Sydney.

**Books by Libby Gleeson include:**

The Necklace and the Present
Go To Sleep, Jessie!
Mum Goes to Work
Dodger
Dear Writer
Red
The Great Bear

Above: Libby Gleeson
Below: Morris Gleitzman

## Morris Gleitzman

Morris Gleitzman writes novels for teenagers and humorous books for younger children. When he writes about serious subjects, like the Holocaust, the characters speak like real children and have all the common cares and joys that even children going through disasters can experience.

**Books by Morris Gleitzman include:**

Once
Then
Now
Soon
After
Loyal Creatures
Aristotle's Nostril
Toad series

## Bob Graham

An award winning author and illustrator of picture books and novels for children. Bob Graham's awards include the Smarties Gold Medal, the Kate Greenaway Medal and CBCA Awards.

**Books by Bob Graham include:**

How to Heal a Broken Wing
Oscar's Half Birthday
Let's Get a Pup
Buffy
April Underhill, Tooth Fairy
Greetings From Sandy Beach
A Bus Called Heaven

# HOW TO WRITE A STORY OF YOUR OWN

## 1. Plot

Briefly work out what will happen in your story. Most stories include a problem and then a solution.

## 2. Characters

Who will be the main characters? Having one main character makes it easier for readers to feel they are part of that character's adventures.

## 3. Setting

Where does the story happen?

## 4. Genre

Most books have a genre, which means they could be science fiction, romance, mysteries, historical stories, school stories, family stories, biographies or many other types of writing.

## 5. Editing

Stories always need lots of editing once they are written. Make your story as perfect as possible.

## 6. Style

Try to mix dialogue with descriptions. A whole book just with dialogue or just with descriptions will be hard to read.

## 7. The Ending

End the story with a climax. This means that something important happens to finish off the story.

## 8. Your Readers

Ask your friends and family to read your story. Fix any mistakes they find.

## 9. Printing

Use a computer to make up a title page as a cover, then print your story, staple the pages together with the cover, and your book is complete! If you don't have a computer, write it all out neatly and draw a cover instead.

## 10.

Hold a book launch so everyone knows that you have written a book.

Above : Andy Griffiths

## Wendy Harmer

Wendy Harmer is a Sydney writer who is also a comedian and a radio announcer. Her Pearlie series for young girls, and her humorous stories about the trials of teenage life, have been very well received by her readers.

**Books by Wendy Harmer include:**

Pearlie series
Ava and Angus series
I Lost My Mobile at the Mall
I Made Lattes for a Love God

## Andy Griffiths

Andy Griffiths writes humorous books with odd and impossible settings, and plots that move everyday surroundings into fantasy locations. His characters are funny, resourceful and good at dealing with all sorts of unusual events. Andy used to be an English teacher and he wrote stories to amuse his students and show them that reading could be fun. The Treehouse and Just series have been so popular that children wait with excitement for the next book to be published. The drawings by Terry Denton do more than just illustrate the stories. They are whimsical cartoons that have a life of their own.

**Books by Andy Griffiths include:**

Treehouse series
Just! series
Schooling Around series
Bad series
Bum series

Above: Libby Hathorn

## YABBA AWARDS (The Young Australians Best Book Award)

Founded in Victoria in 1986, these awards let children choose their favourite Australian book each year.

Above: Sonya Hartnett

## Sonya Hartnett

Sonya Hartnett's novels for teenagers have controversial themes and cover serious topics. She has won the Astrid Lindgren Memorial Award and the Guardian Children's Fiction Prize.

**Books by Sonya Hartnett include:**

Sleeping Dogs
Thursday's Child
The Children of the King
Princes
Forest
The Silver Donkey
Golden Boys

## Libby Hathorn

Libby Hathorn writes picture books, novels and poetry for children and teenagers. The Australian movie, The Echo of Thunder, was based on her novel, Thunderwith. Libby Hathorn began her career as a teacher and librarian.

**Books by Libby Hathorn include:**

A Boy Like Me
The ABC Book of Australian Poetry
A Baby for Loving
Thunderwith
Outside

### ASTRID LINDGREN MEMORIAL AWARD

An international award for children's literature. Winners from Australia were Sonya Hartnett in 2008, and Shaun Tan in 2011.

## Odo Hirsch

Odo Hirsch writes series of adventure stories for young children as well as novels with mystery and fantasy themes for older children.

**Books by Odo Hirsch include:**

Amelia Dee and the Peacock Lamp
Darius Bell series
Will Buster series
Antonio S and the Mystery of Theodore Guzman

## Leigh Hobbs

Leigh Hobbs was appointed the Australian Children's Laureate for 2016 to 2017. As well as illustrating his own books, Leigh Hobbs is also a sculptor and has designed whimsical figures for the Luna Parks in Melbourne and Sydney. His 'Old Tom' character, a sneaky cat who is more like a naughty child than a pet, has been the star of a cartoon series for television.

**Books by Leigh Hobbs include:**

Old Tom series
Mr Chicken series
Horrible Harriet series
Freaks series
Mr Badger series

# E-BOOKS

*How are e-books different from paper books?*

Some include voices that read the text.

A power source is needed before the book can be read.

Some have hyperlinks.

You may be able to change the brightness of the page.

You may be able to change the size of the text.

An e-book device is more fragile than a book.

Some include videos.

Some also highlight each word as it is said by the voice.

# HOW TO WRITE A BOOK REVIEW OF A NOVEL

1. Start by writing the title and author of the book.

2. If you want to be very precise, add the publisher's name and the ISBN code as well.

3. Write a few sentences on the plot, characters and setting of the story.

4. Explain what sort of readers would like this novel.

5. Give your opinion about what you thought of the novel.

## FAST FACT

Every book published needs a unique 13 digit code called an ISBN.

Left: Elizabeth Honey

## Elizabeth Honey

Elizabeth Honey is an author of picture books, poetry and novels for children. She won the CBCA Award for Picture Book of the Year, and her work has been on the Honour Book list a number of times. In her books she likes to break up the text with jokes, pictures and a mixture of typefaces. These all make her stories interesting to read and to look at.

**Books by Elizabeth Honey include:**

Honey Sandwich
45 & 47 Stella Street
Don't Pat the Wombat
Not a Nibble
What Do You Think, Feezal?

## Paul Jennings

Many of Paul Jennings' books are collections of short stories, making them hugely popular with children who find a long novel tedious. His millions of book sales around the world prove that humour with a touch of fantasy are a winning combination in children's stories.

**Books by Paul Jennings include:**
Unreal!
Unseen!
Don't Look Now series
Rascal series
Wicked series (written with Morris Gleitzman)

Above: Catherine Jinks

## Catherine Jinks

Catherine Jinks is a winner of the Victorian Premier's Literature Award and CBCA Awards. Her books often rely on her expert knowledge of medieval history to produce a combination of fantasy, folklore and science fiction.

**Books by Catherine Jinks include:**
City of Orphans series
Genius series
Theophilus Grey series
Pagan series
Allie's Ghost Hunters series

## Barry Jonsberg

Barry Jonsberg writes novels for children and teenagers and is also a teacher. His stories range from mystery and suspense to comedies that follow characters as they make their way through the maze of teenage life.

**Books by Barry Jonsberg include:**
My Life as an Alphabet
Game Theory
Pandora Jones series
The Dog That Dumped on My Doona

Above: Barry Jonsberg

## Robin Klein

Robin Klein's stories have lively characters who like to make their own rules. Hating Alison Ashley puts into words the feelings that many young girls have when they are faced with who is in and who is out in classroom social groups. Robin Klein does not avoid dark themes and places children in the centre of disturbing situations, while giving them the power to triumph.

**Books by Robin Klein include:**

Hating Alison Ashley
People Might Hear You
Halfway Across the Galaxy and Turn Left
Thing
Penny Pollard series

## Sofie Laguna

Sofie Laguna's books include picture books for young children and novels for older children and adults. She is a winner of the Miles Franklin Award.

**Books by Sofie Laguna include:**

On Our Way to the Beach
Our Australian Girl (Grace) series
Do You Dare: Fighting Bones
Bird and Sugar Boy

## Alison Lester

Alison Lester was an Australian Children's Laureate in 2012. She writes children's picture books and chapter books which have themes of preserving the natural environment, and of the joy of caring for pets and domestic animals. Her Bonnie & Sam series is about two young girls who love horses and combine riding and having exciting adventures.

**Books by Alison Lester include:**

Our Island
Are We There Yet?
Noni the Pony
The Magic Beach
Kissed by the Moon
Sophie Scott Goes South
Bonnie & Sam series

Below: Sofie Laguna

## John Marsden

John Marsden writes about dystopian societies and teenagers dealing with difficult lives, oppression and the results of social unrest. His novel, Tomorrow, When the War Began, has been made into a film and television series. He believes that the best way to tell a story about a subject like war or disaster is to concentrate on the lives of a small group of people who are experiencing it. John Marsden is also a teacher and founded the Candlebark school near Melbourne.

**Books by John Marsden include:**

So Much to Tell You
Letters From the Inside
Everything I Know About Writing
Secret Men's Business
The Rabbits
Tomorrow, When the War Began
The Ellie Chronicles
The Year My Life Broke

## David Metzenthen

As a writer of picture books and novels for children and teenagers, David Metzenthen creates a voice for children living in harsh situations. His subjects also investigate the experiences of young soldiers, both in war and after they return home.

**Books by David Metzenthen include:**

Stony Heart Country
Wildlight
Boys of Blood and Bone
Black Water
One Minute's Silence
Dreaming the Enemy

## Glenda Millard

Glenda Millard's picture books and children's stories are a celebration of life and the ways children can overcome adversity. Her Isabella's Garden is a winner of the Speech Pathology Australia Book of the Year.

**Books by Glenda Millard include:**

Isabella's Garden
For All Creatures
Applesauce and the Christmas Miracle
Layla Queen of Hearts

Above: David Metzenthen

# CRAFT ACTIVITY

## Designing a book

An author is the person who writes a book, but there are also others who help make the book look good. These people are called designers. They create the covers and page designs that attract readers.
Here are some craft ideas for making a notebook for yourself.

1. Cut up all your saved gift paper into squares. Staple them together to make a notebook.
2. Collect some plain pieces of paper for your notebook. Use a piece of leather as a cover. Wrap the leather around the pages then sew your notebook together down the spine.
3. Collect a pile of pages then paste craft glue all along one edge of them. Leave to dry and you now have your own notebook from which you can tear off pages.
4. Using the holes made from a hole puncher, tie a piece of ribbon, leather or twine through the holes to keep all the note pages together.
5. Make an eye catching cover for your notebook using one of your own paintings or drawings.
6. Use a computer book creation program to design your notepad.

MY BOOK

## Sally Murphy

Sally Murphy is an award winning writer of picture books, verse novels and textbooks.

**Books by Sally Murphy include:**

Roses Are Blue
Do Not Forget Australia
Toppling
Pearl Verses the World
Meet Mary MacKillop
Australia's Great War: 1915

## Belinda Murrell

Belinda Murrell writes stories for girls about going backwards in time to visit different eras. She has also written picture books and a series of chapter books for younger children.

**Books by Belinda Murrell include:**

Lulu Bell series
The River Charm
The Secret Star
The Locket of Dreams
The Forgotten Pearl
The Ivory Rose

## Narelle Oliver

Narelle Oliver is an artist and the creator of picture books for children. Her artwork has been influenced by the children she taught at the Queensland School for the Deaf. She sometimes uses collage for her pictures, and looks to nature for her inspiration.

**Books by Narelle Oliver include:**

Don't Let A Spoonbill in the Kitchen
Baby Bilby, Where Do You Sleep?
Home
The Very Blue Thingamajig
Mermaids Most Amazing

### AUSTRALIAN CHILDREN'S LAUREATES

2016 & 2017 - Leigh Hobbs
2014 & 2015 - Jackie French
2012 & 2013 - Alison Lester and Boori Monty Pryor

Above: Belinda Murrell
Left: Sally Murphy

Below: Oliver Phommavanh

## Jan Ormerod (1946 - 2013)

Jan Ormerod's picture books concentrate on the daily experiences of children. Through their eyes we see the lives of the adults around them, and the way that children can turn a worrying time, like drought or loneliness, into a fun-filled adventure.

**Books by Jan Ormerod include:**
Lizzie Nonsense
101 Things To Do With a Baby
Water Witcher
Molly and Her Dad
The Swap
Maudie and Bear

## Oliver Phommavanh

An author of very funny books for children and young teenagers. His Thai characters do their best to juggle their Thai home lives, crazy things that happen at school, and the trials of teenage love. Oliver Phommavanh is also a comedian and a teacher.

**Books by Oliver Phommavanh include:**
Punchlines
Rich and Rare
The Other Christy
Stuff Happens: Ethan
Thai-riffic!
Thai-no-mite!

## Boori Monty Pryor

Boori Monty Pryor's books include children's novels and picture books, as well as an autobiography. He travels around Australia and overseas talking about literature and his Aboriginal culture. His picture book, Shake a Leg, is a happy story of dance and sharing amongst all types of people. Boori Monty Pryor was an Australian Children's Laureate in 2012.

**Books by Boori Monty Pryor include:**
Shake a Leg
Flytrap
Maybe Tomorrow
My Girragundji
The Binna Binna Man
Njunjul the Sun

Above: Sally Rippin
Right: Shaun Tan

## Sally Rippin

As the creator of the popular series Billie B. Brown and Hey Jack!, Sally Rippin is one of the most widely read children's authors in Australia. Her characters handle everyday situations with humour and originality. The novels for older children include contributions to the Our Australian Girl series about the lives of children in Australia's past. Angel Creek is a novel for older children that fuses fantasy with the problems of working out what is right and wrong.

**Books by Sally Rippin include:**
Billie B. Brown series
Hey Jack! series
Our Australian Girl: Lina at the Games
Our Australian Girl: A Lesson For Lina
Angel Creek
Polly and Buster

## Emily Rodda

Emily Rodda is best known for her series featuring heroic young characters, magic and fantasy lands. She also writes science fiction for children and uses her own real name, Jennifer Rowe, on her books for adults.

**Books by Emily Rodda include:**
Pigs Might Fly
Deltora Quest series
The Three Doors series
Rowan of Rin series
Rondo series

## Shaun Tan

Shaun Tan's novels and picture books have a surreal quality that allows them to appeal to both children and adults at different levels. He won an Academy Award for an animated film of his book, The Lost Thing.

**Books by Shaun Tan include:**
The Rules of Summer
The Arrival
Takes From Outer Suburbia
The Lost Thing

# HOW TO WRITE A BOOK REVIEW OF A NON-FICTION BOOK

1. Start by writing the title and author of the book.
2. If you want to be very precise, add the publisher's name and the ISBN code as well.

3. Explain what the book is about.
4. Talk about the experience of the author and whether they are qualified to write about the topic.
5. Who is the book written for? Is it written for students or for recreational reading?

6. Does the book contain tables, graphs or labelled pictures?
7. Does the book have an index, a glossary and a list of places to read more about the topic?
8. Now add your comments on whether you thought the book was interesting and useful.

## Nadia Wheatley

Nadia Wheatley's books have themes of the environment, culture and Aboriginal reconciliation. She also writes for adults and has a strong interest in education.

**Books by Nadia Wheatley include:**
My Place
Five Times Dizzy
Australians All
Going Bush
The House That Was Eureka

## Colin Thompson

Colin Thompson's picture books are full of fantasy and adventure and his novels turn hauntings and magic into tales of laughter. The Floods series is about a family of witches and wizards and their quirky and very funny exploits.

**Books by Colin Thompson include:**
The Floods series
The Dragons series
The Paperbag Prince
Pictures of Home
Looking For Atlantis
Castle Twilight
Space The Final Effrontery

Above: Nadia Wheatley
Left: Colin Thompson

## Bruce Whatley

Bruce Whatley writes and illustrates his own picture books, and has also illustrated books for some of Australia's leading writers. His own books are often based on his family life and pets.

**Books by Bruce Whatley include:**
The Ugliest Dog in the World
Looking for Crabs
Detective Donut

Above: Margaret Wild

## Claire Zorn

Claire Zorn writes novels for teenagers, and both her first and second novels have won awards.

**Books by Claire Zorn include:**

The Sky So Heavy
The Protected
One Would Think the Deep

### KOALA AWARDS
### (Kids' Own Australian Literature Award)

The KOALA Awards are chosen by children who send in their votes from across New South Wales each year. The first award was presented in 1987.

## Margaret Wild

Margaret Wild writes picture books, verse novels for teenagers and stories for children. She worked as a book editor in children's publishing before writing her own books.

**Books by Margaret Wild include:**

There's a Sea in My Bedroom
Jinx
One Night
Itsy-Bitsy Babies
Itsy-Bitsy Animals
The Stone Lion
Lucy Goosey
Bogtrotter

Above: Claire Zorn

# Glossary

| WORD | MEANING |
|---|---|
| accolade | praise |
| caricature | exaggerated description of a character's traits |
| dilemma | problem |
| dyslexic | having problems with reading and spelling |
| dystopia | fictional society that is suffering destruction |
| exotic | unusual and foreign |
| folklore | traditional community stories |
| format | the way a book is arranged and constructed |
| hyperlink | used in an electronic document to go to another section |
| jostle | push roughly |
| medieval | from the Middle Ages |
| oppression | unjust treatment by those more powerful |
| poignant | sad and regretful |
| portrayal | depiction in writing or art |
| renowned | famous and praiseworthy |
| tedious | boring |
| trailblazer | first to do something new |
| turmoil | trouble and upset |
| typeface | design of letters and numbers used in printing |
| whimsical | funny and cute |

**WHERE TO FIND OUT MORE**

www.thelitcentre.org.au
www.australia.gov.au/about-australia/australian-story/austn-childrens-books
www.childrenslaureate.org.au
www.cbca.org.au